Dot &
Jabber

and the Mystery of the Missing Stream

Ellen Stoll Walsh

Green Light Readers

HOUGHTON MIFFLIN HARCOURT

Boston New York

The illustrations in this book are cut-paper collage.
The display type was set in Berkeley Oldstyle Medium.
The text type was set in Berkeley Oldstyle Book.

The Library of Congress has cataloged the hardcover edition as follows:
Walsh, Ellen Stoll.
Dot & Jabber and the mystery of the missing stream/written and illustrated by Ellen Stoll Walsh.
p. cm.
"Companion book to Dot & Jabber and the great acorn mystery."
Summary: Two mice investigate why the stream dried up after a big storm.
[1. Rivers—Fiction. 2. Dams—Fiction. 3. Mice—Fiction.] 1. Title.
PZ7.W1675Dq 2002
[E]—dc21   2001005262

ISBN: 978-0-15-216512-3 hardcover
ISBN: 978-0-544-79166-4 GLR paper over board
ISBN: 978-0-544-79167-1 GLR paperback

Manufactured in Malaysia
TWP 10 9 8 7 6 5 4 3 2 1

4500594153

For Leila and David

The detectives couldn't believe their eyes. Leaves and branches were everywhere!

"There is no mystery about this mess," said Dot. "The storm last night nearly blew me away."

"I bet the stream is really full," said Jabber. "Let's go float some sticks."

"Sorry," hissed a snake. "You are too late. The stream is empty. Come and see."

The mice hurried after the snake.
"It's empty, all right," said Dot.
"There are just a few puddles left.
When did you see the water last?"

"During the storm. At first the rain made the water deep. Then slowly, slowly, it disappeared." The snake sighed. "Can you find it?"

"We've never looked for lost water before," said Jabber.

"Let's look upstream," said Dot.
"That's where the water comes from—
when there *is* water."

The detectives followed the stream bed.

After a while they came to a puddle crowded with minnows, all bumping into each other. "Excuse me—Sorry— Beg your pardon—"

"This is what's left of our stream since the storm last night," a minnow complained. "It's hardly big enough for all of us."

"We're looking for your missing water," said Dot. "Until we find it, why don't you all try swimming around in the same direction?"

"Good idea," said the minnows.
"Which way? This way—Sorry—
Excuse me—"

The detectives walked and walked.

"I'm tired of climbing over sticks," said Jabber.

"I think these sticks might be clues!" said Dot. "They blew down at about the same time the stream disappeared."

"Then I'm tired of climbing over *clues*," said Jabber. "How can a stick make water go away?"

"That's part of the mystery," said Dot.

Some crayfish were waiting by a puddle.

"We're taking turns," they told the mice. "Turtle is in there now. Before the stream disappeared, there was plenty of room for everyone. Now look what we have—leaves and branches. We can't swim in leaves and branches!"

"Leaves and branches are everywhere," said Dot. "We think they are clues to the missing-water mystery."

"We just don't know how the clues fit together," said Jabber.

"Oh, Jabber," said Dot. "I think you've done it! One branch can't stop a stream, but lots of them put together might."

"I get it!" said Jabber. "Like the dams the beavers make."

"Yes," said Dot. "Only without the beavers."

"Come on!" said Jabber. "Let's go see if we're right." The mice raced upstream.

At last they found it—a magnificent dam made of many branches jammed together.

"Well, Jabber, we've done it again," said Dot. "Another mystery solved by the great mouse detectives."

"The clues fit, that's for sure,"
said Jabber. "But we have one more
problem. The water is still stuck."

Twigs snapped. Branches cracked.
The dam bulged and groaned.

"Look out, Jabber! Now our
problem is to get out of here fast!"
yelled Dot.

They scrambled up the bank just as the mighty dam split apart. The water tumbled over itself in its rush to fill the stream bed.

The two tired mouse detectives sat on the bank and watched the stream flow past.

"I suppose we should start back," said Dot.

"Let's put some of those clues together and make a raft," said Jabber. "We came all this way to find the water. Now it can take us home."

More About Storms and Dams

During a storm, the wind can blow branches and leaves out of trees and onto the ground—and sometimes into a stream. The sticks can pile up and the leaves can wedge between them, forming a barrier that holds the water back. Anything that blocks the flow of water is called a *dam*.

When branches dam a stream, the animals and fish downstream can't get enough water. They may be left with shallow puddles like the minnows and the crayfish Dot and Jabber meet, or they may have no water at all!

As the mice discover (just in time!), the water pushing against the dam creates pressure. The force of the water builds up and breaks the dam apart, allowing the stream to flow freely once again.

Although Dot and Jabber's dam was caused by a storm, other kinds of dams are built on purpose. Beavers cut down trees and use them to build dams across streams. The dams hold the water back and create ponds, where the beavers make lodges out of sticks and mud. There they raise their young and store food for winter. People build concrete dams across rivers for many reasons: to hold water for drinking or watering crops, to make lakes for fishing and boating, and to store water for generating electric power. These dams are designed to let water flow through to the creatures downstream.

How did Dot and Jabber figure out that a dam was the answer to the mystery of the missing stream? The mouse detectives knew that in nature, things that seem unrelated actually can be connected. You just need to follow the clues: storm + stream + sticks + leaves = a dam!